Richard Stephenson

4/29/2000

Kim Marshall

THE WAR OF THE MORMON COW

CRAZY HORSE CHRONICLES

BY RICHARD JEPPERSON

THE WAR
OF THE MORMON COW

BEING THE FIRST PART OF THE

CRAZY HORSE CHRONICLES

BY

RICHARD JEPPERSON
ILLUSTRATED BY KEN MUNDIE
FORWARD BY JACK HEMINGWAY

String of Beads Publications
Park City, Utah

THE WAR OF THE MORMON COW:
BEING THE FIRST PART OF THE CRAZY HORSE CHRONICLES
Richard Jepperson

Published by STRING OF BEADS PUBLICATIONS
P.O. Box 1673
Park City, Utah 84060

Copyright © 1999 Richard Jepperson.
Illustrations: Ken Mundie
Cover design: Ken Mundie
Forward: Jack Hemingway

Library of Congress Catalog Card Number: 99-90506

ISBN 0-9672012-0-9

Printed and bound in the United States of America

First Printing July 1999

10 9 8 7 6 5 4 3 2 1

In Memory of:

Mahto Sica (Bad Bear), a.k.a. Chaske Wicks

Born: May 9, 1925 - Crossed over: February 8, 1994

*My pathfinder through the labyrinth of
the history and legends of The People, we call Sioux.*

FOREWORD

Perhaps the most difficult writing of all involves attempts to turn legend into a reality we can perceive. To begin with the writer must steep himself completely in the legend so that it becomes real to him. Having done so he then must visualize the events of the legend and portray them in a manner understandable to his audience. This little segment of the history of our native people and of their relationship with the white outsiders is an eye opener for anyone who reads it. Richard Jepperson has accomplished a formidable task and embellished it in great part with the aid of the magnificent drawings of his gifted illustrator, Ken Mundie. The reader will find the story and its characters, the young Crazy Horse and Black Robe Woman coming to life as he reads and then achieving a visual reality as he absorbs the beauty of the illustrations. We can only hope there will not be too long a wait for the second and third chronicles.

Jack Hemingway
Sun Valley, Idaho

I thought again of the string of beads in my vision. There were bright beads and dull beads and plump beads and shriveled beads. There were beads that glowed with life and dark beads that ate the light.

- Crazy Horse -

The War of the Mormon Cow is the story of Black Robe Woman and Crazy Horse, in their youth. She called him Curly and he called her Little Mouse.

PREFACE

Curly's best friends' were Little Mouse, a bossy, shinny eyed girl a few years younger and Lone Bear, a loud mouthed big brother type who could beat up anyone near his age and often did. The three were always together. They called him Curly to make fun of his light, wavy hair. Curly seldom got angry or pouted or blamed someone else. In spite of the bossy girl and bullying buddy he usually got his way. Not because he was tougher, or had a smarter mouth, but because he was always one step ahead. He had that complex quality, found in born leaders, we call charisma. Curly wasn't a carefree boy for very long. On the 19th day of August of 1854, at twelve years of age, he was caught up in **THE WAR OF THE MORMON COW** and rode through acrid smoke, whirring bullets and thrumming cannon balls to rescue Little Mouse.

This story is written in the meter and structure of the Sioux language, as Crazy Horse would have told it. It is mostly true but when history and legend conflict I choose legend, where the spirit of the Sioux still lives.

- Richard Jepperson -

THE DAY OF THE RED DAWN

The day dawned with a sky as red as the coals of a fire. A very bad sign. The smoke from the lodge fires rose straight up then flattened into a haze over the camp of a thousand lodges. It was late summer and we were camped since spring to receive the annuities promised by the Peace Paper. By the time the day wind whispered to the night wind and left, only one lodge remained.

Everyone knew there would be great trouble. Lodges were pulled down and laced for travel. There was a great milling of people, women, children, old ones, horses, travois and dogs. Little Thunder rode back and forth across the Shell River marking a path through the quicksand with standing poles of willows. Only the lodge of the wounded and dying Conquering Bear stood, guarded by the men of his Akacita. The night wind whispered fitfully and jerked at the lodge flap.

The flickering fire cast shadows of caregivers onto the lodge skin. Man Afraid, Big Partisan and Ice, the strange and powerful medicine man, stayed with Conquering Bear, who was the Peace Chief that had placed his mark on the Peace Paper at the Big Council and talked long for others to do so. Now he lay with a great wound in his stomach, a leg torn off and his side leaking yellow blood.

Ahead, in the dark, the whole of the Lakotas traversed north. It had been a day to remember. The happenings raced back and forth in my mind...

WAITING FOR THE ANNUITIES

When we first gathered at Fort Laramie it was good. Every year since the Peace Paper we would rendezvous in the spring. There was much trading and dancing and meeting with old friends. But this year it was near summer's end and each day the old ones looked to the east waiting for the agent of the Washington Father. Every day it was asked, "Will he come to-day?" and no one seemed to know. "Winter comes soon and we will starve if we don't get our presents."

The day before the day of the red dawn Lone Bear, Little Mouse and I hid in the grass and watched a Mormon on the trail beating an old cow with bleeding feet. The cow spooked, flipped its tail and ran into the Brule camp. It ran kicking its back legs up, scattering travois and parfleches, knocking down one lodge then got stuck with its horns in the skins of another.

The Mormon chased after the cow until he saw the great Indian camp. Straight Foretop, a Minneconjou, waved and shouted to the Mormon to come and get his cow. But the man left the cow, to pay for the trouble. It was of little value because it was old and dry and had bleeding feet. Straight Foretop killed the cow and we ate it.

5

There was much talking and laughing of how the cow ran through the camp and how the Mormon walked backwards, like a *heyoka* dancer, and waved his stick then tripped and fell and got up and ran away. I was given a piece of the skin for my new war club.

Conquering Bear and Man Afraid smoked and talked into the fire late that night. They thought there might be a little trouble so they said, "Let us go to the fort and talk with the Soldier Chief in the morning." The next morning started with the red dawn, a very bad sign. They met in council to decide what to do and Conquering Bear prepared to go to the fort.

Before they could leave the Soldier Chief of the fort, called Grattan, came with thirty soldiers and two wagon-guns.

There was a small village and trading post nearby owned by a Frenchman called Bat. He was little, squat and hairy, with a Brule wife and a friend of the Sioux for more years than the fort had stood. That morning, at the fort, Bat had talked with the Soldier Chief and offered the Mormon ten dollars for the cow, of his own money, to avoid trouble. But the Mormon wanted twenty-five dollars and Bat said he would not pay that much for a strong cow. Bat smelled trouble and would not come with him, nor would the Mormon.

Grattan left Bat and came to camp with Wyuse, demanding the cow killer. Conquering Bear, Man Afraid, Big Partisan and the brother of Conquering Bear, wrapped in council blankets, met Grattan and offered the council pipe. Grattan said, "No."

Little Mouse pushed through the people and stood behind Conquering Bear.

Wyuse was the American-to-Indian speaker. He was always drunk and lied but the Soldier Chief would use no other. When Wyuse talked to the council he made signs of throwing green buffalo chips in their face. He said he was a strong enemy of the Sioux and he would bring them down, cut their hearts out and eat them.

Conquering Bear and Man Afraid went back and forth between the Soldier Chief and Straight Foretop, trying to get Straight Foretop to surrender or the Soldier Chief to wait until the agent of the Father came to say what should be done. Straight Foretop would not go with the soldiers over the killing of an old cow. Conquering Bear then offered a good mule and sent the camp crier to get more from the tribes and the crier returned with five sticks, meaning five good horses, and placed them on the ground before the Soldier Chief even though the cow was worth nothing.

Grattan wanted to put Straight Foretop in the iron house and demanded that Conquering Bear make the Minneconjou come. Conquering Bear could not make him do that because Straight Foretop was a guest. Each time Conquering Bear said, "Wait, wait," and asked to sit and smoke and settle the trouble, Wyuse changed the words and Grattan got redder in the face.

The last thing said by Wyuse caused Grattan to roar in defiance, his freckled face glowing red. Wyuse turned away and the Soldier Chief pulled his long knife and shouted and the soldiers fired at Conquering Bear and the others, who stood wrapped in council blankets.

THE WAR OF THE MORMON COW

It seemed but an eye blink since the Soldier Chief, standing in the middle of the council circle, shouted and his thirty soldiers fired their wagon guns and the brother of Conquering Bear fell dead and his blood splashed Little Mouse. Grattan again called out and the wagon guns roared and Conquering Bear fell, wounded.

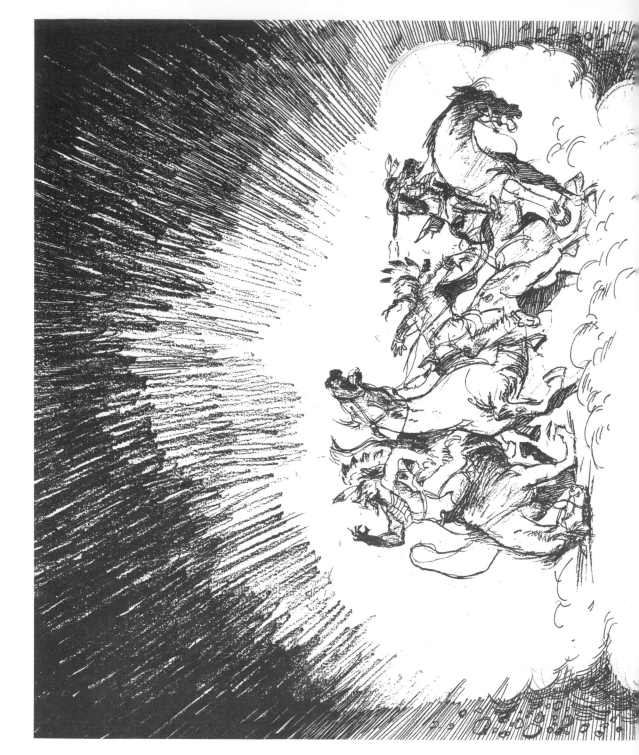

17

I jumped on my pony and rode through clouds of foul smelling black smoke and fire and whirring cannon balls to lift up Little Mouse.

Straight Foretop lifted his rifle and fired and Grattan fell. Spotted Tail whooped and a hundred warriors shot a flood of arrows into the soldiers at the wagon guns. With lances and war clubs they charged like a buffalo herd trampling the soldiers into the ground, grabbing their guns and swinging them like clubs on the rest.

More warriors than you could count came from every direction, crying war whoops, kicking their ponies, leaning forward, waving lances, clubs and axes. As Little Mouse and I galloped for the Oglala camp we saw a few soldiers get away. They tried to stand and fight but they were soon dead.

Warriors jumped off ponies swinging axes and war clubs until all the soldiers lay on the ground naked and bloody. They jumped back on their ponies, standing high in stirrups as they raced in a whooping circle waving blue coats, pants, soldier guns, black boots and scalps.

We were too young to ride with warriors but our blood rose and we too circled and whooped, singing war songs. My brother, He Dog, saw us and joined in the victory parade.

All over an old cow with bleeding feet!

Little Mouse and I were at the edge of the camp near the trail to the fort and we saw the drunken Iowa, Wyuse, turn and race to the ridge where, only the day before, we hid in the grass to watch the Mormon train go by. At the sound of the first shot Wyuse, gasping in fear, turned his horse and spurred toward the fort. Brules were hard after him. Oglalas swept from the right across the trail in front to cut him off. Wyuse pulled to his left, hoping to outrun the hooting warriors. His horse stumbled and fell, pinning his left leg.

Jerking his trapped leg free from the squirming mass of horseflesh, he scrambled, limping, stumbling and crawling into the Brule death lodge of Bull Tail for sanctuary. Three Brule warriors entered and pulled him from the sacred place, bawling and kicking like a cow-calf.

Wyuse's own wife's brother struck him with his war club, tore off his clothes, cut a long gash on each leg from ankle to waist and left him screaming in pain outside the death lodge. One-by-one each of the warriors strode up. They cursed his name as they pierced him with

lance, slashed him with knife or smashed with their club. No one took his scalp.

After they left, Little Mouse and I sneaked up feeling strange and sick. We stood over Wyuse, blood already clotting like dark red pitch, his face contorted forever in fear and pain. His eyes stuck out like they never fit in his head. My blood rose as I looked down on him. For a moment I was a warrior. I raised my fists and cried to the sky, "Kii, Kii; Yii, Yii, Yii." It was good to kill the enemies of my people. But he was already dead. Little Mouse pulled me away to race to the Oglala camp as the battle raged.

There were Americans at Bat's Post who rode along with the soldiers from the fort but had not joined in the fight. They had stood on the roofs and watched the fight. They could no longer be seen. "Where are the rabbits hiding? Shake the brush, scare them out!" the young Brules, their bodies shining with sweat and streaked with paint and blood, cried as they went from house to house. Bat ran along side, wringing his hands, pleading, "They have done nothing these Americans. They are blameless."

"They are the enemy," the nephew of Conquering Bear shouted as he plunged the long knife taken from a dead soldier into bedrolls and through strawricks. He Dog and I joined the great Minneconjou-Oglala warrior, called Hump. Hump had chosen me for his little brother to teach when I was just able to run and ride a pony.

The young warriors racing about and shouting to go back and raid the fort and kill everyone and take the goods for our annuities. More and more said, "Yes" to that as they thought of the long winter without supplies. When Bat heard them he ran about shouting, "No, no." If you attack the fort then next year the Father of all Soldier Chiefs will send more Bluecoats than all the pebbles in the creek and they will hunt you and kill all the warriors and all your women and children and the Sioux will be no more.

The warriors were angry at what Bat said so he gave them some jerky and molasses and coffee, but they would not listen and before it was over he gave them all he had, opening his storage and giving it out until he had nothing left. But the warriors wanted more and they talked of the Gratiot houses where the stores of the Hudson Bay company had stood without guard every year for more than the life of a man, because they had always honored every agreement with the Indian. All the chiefs were against such a thing. It would be a great dishonor. Red Leaf spoke against it as did Spotted Tail and Hump.

Red Leaf pulled off his blanket showing the scars of many sun dances on his breast and said, "I am a Lakota warrior like you and am the brother of Conquering Bear. Do not touch these goods. Trouble enough has been brought upon The People. Leave here in peace and go to the hunting grounds. Go fast and make plenty of meat and robes for winter."

These were good words. I was there to hear him say them. Many called out, "Hoye!" But the war blood was still in the hearts of the warriors and they pushed past Red Leaf, put their shoulders to the door. When it broke the leaders crowded into the storeroom and handed out the goods. Little Mouse and I were among them, racing back and forth to get things and load and pack the horses.

Everything was taken and the storehouses stood empty. We later found that whiskey was stored under the floorboards but no one knew it then. Hump and Swift Bear, the brother of Bat's wife, now spoke for Bat and harangued the wild young men. They listened because Swift Bear was as strong among the Brule as Hump was among the Oglala and Minneconjou. They went away like dogs caught at the meat racks, looking back over their shoulders, wanting more but afraid of a beating.

MOVING NORTH

Once the trouble started the great camp dissolved like sugar in a rainstorm.

There was now a great river of men, women, children, dogs, horses and travois moving north under a cloud of dust stretching over many miles.

The Oglalas, the Brules and Minneconjou went together.

My father, Hump, Man Afraid, other chiefs and Ice, the holy man, made a covered sling for Conquering Bear and carried him gently on their shoulders, walking fast enough to keep ahead of the people with horses and travois, even in rain storms.

They put up his lodge each night. Little Mouse and I tried to look but only Ice, the medicine man, and great warriors could see him. Conquering Bear wanted to get the people far from the fort, for the soldiers would certainly come against us. We traveled all night and the next day. We made camp on the second night. Conquering Bear did not die. He sent my father to lead us north.

That night we were all tired but could not sleep. The warriors talked war around the fire. I lay on my side holding my head in my hand, elbow in the sand, outside the circle with He Dog, Lone Bear and the Pretty One. Sometimes when one spoke well Lone Bear and I jumped up, whooped, waved our clubs and danced. A young Minneconjou of great war-honors stood and said,

"These are strangers in our land. Our land is the Smokey Hill in the south and the Bear Paw in the north, the Black Hills in the east and the Snake in the west. We are the Sioux and have taken this land from the Crow, the Shoshoni, the Piaute and the Pawnee and it is now ours.

"The Americans are as thistles and the Sioux as the north wind. If they so much as prick our toe we will puff a small puff and blow them away forever. It is time to sharpen the knives and axes of war and drive these Americans from our hunting grounds forever."

Lightning flashed and crashed and the night sky rumbled as if to say, "Hoye, Hoye," honoring what the Minneconjou said.

He Dog, Lone Bear and I talked with other not-yet-warriors on the edge of the circle. We talked of doing great things, stealing Pawnee horses and counting coup on the Crow and the Snake. Then the old women would sing our names and the young girls smile as we rode by, as they had for Red Cloud, Pawnee Killer, Black Twin and Hump.

Little Mouse joined our circle and said, "You are just talking big. You can no longer do these things." And Pretty One, who was sitting upright so as not to get his white buckskin shirt dirty, said, "There is no longer any horse taking and no warpath. It is against the Peace Paper signed at the Big Council, just peaceful living, smoking and drinking coffee around the fort with the American."

"Hear Pretty One's words," They laughed. "We just killed the soldiers while you walked in beaded buckskin by the women's camp at the fort. You were not at the fight. It would dirty your shirt." So the talk went past Pretty One as it always did.

Pretty One was learning the language of the Americans and spent much time at the fort. He could fight well if he wanted. Five days ago Lone Bear and I tripped him and smeared him with cow dung. He struck back quick and strong and took my war club from me and threw it in the river. I searched the river bottom all day and could not find it. It had been made for me by Hump two years ago and Little Mouse had adorned the handle with copper buttons last winter. I made a new club but I needed leather for binding. That is why I needed a piece from the skin of the Mormon cow.

After many days we reached the Running Water country. It was a good fall. There were bushes of chokecherries, currants and plums. Rabbit, quail, duck; curlew and prairie chicken were easy to catch. We set up camp to stay for the winter.

CURLY'S VISION

In the winter camp one afternoon Lone Bear, Little Mouse and I stood close to Hump as he lifted the Great Chief into the lodge. We stooped down and looked under the lodge skin and saw that Conquering Bear had become a skull with yellow skin still on and eyeholes deep and empty. It was a sacred thing and made me run to my pony to get away by myself. When Little Mouse tried to follow I drove her back.

I looked for a high point where I knew Roan Mule had made an eagle catcher pit. I hobbled my pony so he could graze and water himself, then stripped down to my breechcloth and stretched out in the gravel of the pit and looked at the deep blue of the sky. I thought of things that had happened the last days, seasons and summers.

I thought and began to see that all things were strung together like beads of a necklace, one after another, from this day back and this day forward they went on forever; the hunt, the warpath, the teaching by Hump and my father and the wounding of Conquering Bear.

I thought of other beads: The songs of my mother as we laughed together when I was a child, the songs I sang to Little Mouse as I brushed away the mosquitoes and gnats from her face as she lay in her cradleboard. And how I told her stories until she fell to sleep. I saw the face of Little Mouse as she is now, with her long eyelashes flicking up and down over her smiling, soft brown eyes.

All through that day and into the night I stayed awake, putting sharp stones between my toes and piles of pebbles under my back so I would roll off if I fell asleep. I waited for a vision that should come to understand all things. For two days and nights I stayed awake, my tongue big with thirst, my eyes burning, I shivered in the night. I tried to sing but could not.

I looked at myself in the signal mirror that hung on the rawhide around my neck. When white women at the fort looked at me they had pointed and said a word, "Captive." I asked father what it meant. I became angry when he told me but he said not to worry of what stupid Americans said. I was his son, and he was Oglala and Minneconjou; and my mother was the sister of Spotted Tail, a Brule. I had no white blood no matter what was said. There was no reason for any one to lie since there was no shame for a Lakota women if she wanted a man other than her husband. It was her right to have any man to her bed and she would not hide it as he had heard American women do.

When the third day dawned I tried to lift my mind to another land as I had heard others tell happened to them in their visions, but I became dizzy and could not think. I decided it was enough. I rose and clambered out of the pit and went to look for my pinto.

I found him by a broad cottonwood tree, nickering and tossing his head as I approached. I was dizzy and too weak to remove the hobbles so I sat down with my back against the brown bark of the cottonwood, new fallen dried leaves crunching under me.

I lay my head back, eyes closed, rubbing my scalp side to side on the bark just for the feeling of it. The sounds of chirping katydids and the thrum of a grasshopper made me realize that I had heard no such sounds as I sat in the pit for three days, nor had any insect, bird or squirrel entered or passed by the pit. I breathed deeply, pulling in the smell of distant rain and lightning.

I heard the wind sing to the swaying high branches of the cottonwood as they dipped and flowed as a dance between the tree and the wind. It was as if I had returned to mother earth from another world and she wanted to hold me to her bosom and whisper in my ear. The broad jagged edge leaves rustled, a few of the very high ones had turned red and orange and rattled, but most were still green; dark on the top and silver-green on the under side. The breath of my body flowed as a ghost into the trunk of the tree and I fell asleep.

Suddenly a monster of the dark attacked me from nowhere, great jaws closed on my shoulder and it shook me as a dog worries a tough piece of meat. An angry voice roared, "Where have you been? Why didn't you tell us you were going?"

It was my father, shaking me. Ice stood near. It was near dark and they were angry. They said that this is not the time to be off alone with Crow and Pawnee raiding parties near and perhaps even soldiers coming, everyone worried over the dying chief and no one knowing where I had gone. I told them that I had come to fast for a vision and they were angrier than before. Ice said I could not fast for a vision without preparation and guidance from a wise one, without a sweat and without telling my family.

Back at the lodge I was given soup and wrapped in sleeping robes like a child. I had seen my vision as I slept against the cottonwood but it was not a time they would listen so I would keep it secret until a better time.

That night I heard Little Mouse call, softly. I crawled from my lodge without waking my father and mother. Ice was with her and he motioned us to follow to the lodge of Conquering Bear.

Conquering Bear greeted us in a strong voice but we could not see him. His fire made shadows and light dance on the lodge skin as he told us of sacred things that we must endure together, alone. It made our hearts ache with fear and deep sorrow as he told us of the dark days to come.

He said there would be a time when we must be as two fires in the night and guide our people in the darkest of days. He said we must tell no one of his words and speak only to Ice of the happenings of this night.

Next morning, at daybreak, the herald came for Man Afraid to go to the lodge of Conquering Bear. Now it was time. The other headmen of the Oglalas and the Brules were there. When they came in the Great Chief called to Man Afraid in a voice they could scarcely hear. Such a small voice from the chief who had filled the camp with roaring so even the dogs ran for the hills.

When Man Afraid was near he told him to always remember the treaty of the Big Council. The treaty was of things that belonged to their children, goods to be sent them for giving up the wars on their enemies and for making the trail by the fort a Holy Road where no one who walked on the Road would be killed. There were annuities for fifty-five years and protection by the soldiers for all people, from every enemy, Indian or White.

"It was the American soldiers who came to our peaceful village," one growled. The great chief said there had been a mistake and he did not want Spotted Tail, Red Leaf and Long Chin to get angry at the Americans when he was dead. "There were wild young men among the Sioux who did not do right, too. I am killed and in my place I give my people to Man Afraid, all the Teton Lakotas I give him."

"No, no! I am not strong enough to carry this thing," the Hunkpatila cried out, tears in his eyes.

But Conquering Bear's ears were closed forever and it would be so.

The heralds ran through the camp telling of the passing of Conquering Bear, great wails of grief rose like a snake through the camp, following the path of the herald until the world was filled with the sound.

THE TREATY OF THE HOLY ROAD

And now Conquering Bear was no more. It was he who had signed the Peace Paper for the American's Holy Road and had talked strong to get other chiefs to sign. The Soldier Chief asked that all the tribes would not attack wagons, horses and people on the Holy Road as they passed through, going to the setting sun. There was much talking: Some said, yes! Some said, no! An Oglala of great war-honors rose to speak. "My friends," he said, "These soldiers of the Americans who have pushed into our country with their wagon guns are not many. They are only a few, a puff of breath in the middle of the dark cloud that is our warriors."

"Hoye," the others cried in the sign of agreement. "Hoye, Hoye! It is a good day to gather up the arrows, to sharpen up the knives of war and drive out the soldiers." Others said, "What could it hurt? There would be much feasting and dancing and presents for everybody, a wagon train full. And if the chiefs would touch the pen to the peace paper, there would be presents every summer, for fifty-five years, the age of a strong man." Conquering Bear said that the trail was only a little thing, as wide as the ground between the wheel tracks and that the soldiers were too few to hurt and they took the pen.

The Road started with a little stream of men passing through. The Indian lifted his hand in welcome and went out to smoke. Then the little stream grew to a great river, wider than a man with a strong bow could shoot an arrow across. The stream moved past day after day, always toward the setting sun. The Indian smoked the pipe and wondered which trail they took back. They must be the same ones each year, for there could not be that many people on all the earth.

At first there were only men but now women and children came. The women with pale, sick skins and break-in-two-bodies; the young ones pale too, with hair light and soft as the flying seed of the cottonwood that tickles the nose in summer.

Now we had war because of the Mormon cow on The Road and Conquering Bear, who had signed the Peace Paper, was no more.

ACKNOWLEDGEMENTS

The three parts of the <u>Crazy Horse Chronicles:</u> <u>The War of the Mormon Cow</u>, <u>Pebbles in a Creek</u> and <u>Two Fires in the Night</u> follow the life and legend of Black Robe Woman and Crazy Horse.

Historical sources include <u>The Killing of Chief Crazy Horse</u> by Robert A. Clark; the writings of Eleanor Hinman, as recorded by Mari Sandoz in, <u>Crazy Horse, The Strange Man of the Oglala</u>; and <u>Black Elk Speaks,</u> by John G. Neihardt (Flaming Rainbow).

History tells us little about the women of the Sioux, except for sex and servitude. What we know was written from the memories of old men, a half-century after the happening.

I call on the freedom of story telling, in the tradition of *The Old Ways*, to right a very old wrong and put the woman back where she belongs. Black Robe, the greatest of the Warrior Women, rode side-by-side with Crazy Horse.

My guide through the legends of the Sioux was Chaske Wicks (Bad Bear) and after his passing, his daughter, Winona Johnson.

The talented pen of Ken Mundie brings the story of Black Robe Woman and Crazy Horse to life. Ken is from the "Old" Disney Studios where magic is magical; love is lovable and characters, no matter how fanciful, are believable.